I0519964

Boy ISLAND

HOT GAY EROTICA

CHRIS JOHNS

WARNING

This book contains sexually explicit scenes and adult language. It may be considered offensive to some readers. This book is for sale to adults ONLY.

* * * * * * * * * * * * * * * * * * *

Please store your files wisely where they cannot be accessed by underage readers.

Please feel free to send me an email. Just know that these emails are filtered by my publisher. Good news is always welcome.

Chris Johns - **chris_johns@awesomeauthors.org.**

You might also want to check my blog for Updates and interesting info.
http://chris-johns.awesomeauthors.org/

Copyright © 2014 by Chris Johns
All Rights reserved under International and Pan-American Copyright Conventions. By payment of required fees you have been granted the non-exclusive, non-transferable right to access and read the text of this book. No part of this text may be reproduced, transmitted, downloaded, decompiled, reverse-engineered or stored in or introduced into any information storage and retrieval system, in any form or by any means, whether electronic or mechanical, now known, hereinafter invented, without express written permission of 4Fun Publishing. For more information contact 4Fun Publishing. The publisher does not have any control over and does not assume any responsibility for author or third-party websites or their content. This book is a work of fiction. The characters, incidents and dialogue are drawn from the author's imagination and are not to be construed as real. While reference might be made to actual historical events or existing locations, the names, characters, places and incidents are either products of the author's imagination or are used fictitiously, and any resemblance to actual persons living or dead, business establishments, events or locales is entirely coincidental.

About the Publisher
4Fun Publishing, a member of **BLVNP Incorporated**, 340 S. Lemon #6200, Walnut CA 91789, info@blvnp.com / legal@blvnp.com
NOTE: Due to the highly emotional reaction of some people to works of erotic fiction, any email sent to the above address that contains foul language or religious references is automatically deleted by our anti-spam software and will not be seen. All other communications are welcome.

DISCLAIMER
Please don't be stupid and kill yourself. This book is a work of FICTION. Do not try any new sexual practice that you find in this book. It is fiction and not to be confused with reality. Neither the author nor the publisher or its associates assume any responsibility for any loss, injury, death or legal consequences resulting from acting on the contents in this book. Every character in this book is over 18 years of age. The author's opinions are not to be construed as the opinions of the publisher. The material in this book is for entertainment purposes ONLY. Enjoy.

BOY ISLAND
Hot Gay Erotica

By: Chris Johns

© **Chris Johns 2014**
ISBN: 978-1-62761-921-9

Chapter 1

Topha wandered round in a daze looking at all his new surroundings. He could see no one else and wondered if he had been dropped in this place to rot. The judge had been quite specific or so he thought.

"You will be deposited on Boy Island for a period of two years. If you survive you will be integrated back into society for a second chance."

He had no idea where this 'Boy Island 'was. The nice thing about it though was the temperature. It was only February but he was naked apart from a little pair of shorts. Obviously tropical, with swaying palms and beautiful white sand beaches. How bad could this place get? Was he going to have to survive here alone though or were there other boys similar to him? Where was he going to live? How was he going to survive? He had no tools, nothing to catch fish or game, not that he would have had a clue how to use it anyway.

Having explored a little way along the beach from where he was dropped, he found a bridge over a river running parallel to the coast. Good sign, someone must have built it. He wandered across and into the jungle along a barely discernable path. A few hundred yards and he was in a clearing, dominated by an enclosure of some kind made of wood, spiked poles actually making it look a lot like an old frontier fort from the days of the Indian wars. He expected to see the gates open and a cavalry patrol ride out. He sniggered, *Fantasy land* he thought. But the gates did open and a group of boys, almost the same age as himself, emerged. He noted all wore loincloths of some material and carried spears with knives pushed into the waist band of their loincloths. They also maintained a regular formation with their leader out in front. When they got close, the leader said something and they split into two and surrounded Topha. Once he was encircled, the leader stepped forward.

"Who are you and where have you come from?"

"My name is Topha Lewis, I'm from Boston, but have been sent to Boy Island for two years."

The leader looked round his group. They were all laughing.

"Oh dear, you must have been a naughty boy, no one survives for two years unless they are very good. Are you going to be very good Topha Lewis?"

Topha looked slightly bemused.

"I don't see that I can be much else here unless there is more habitation."

"Oh, there's more habitation, they call themselves 'The Premier Clan', if they catch any of our group they torture them, just for fun, but they make them take a very long time to die. We let them have a victim sometimes, someone who is uncooperative. Are you going to be cooperative Topha?"

"I guess. I want to get back to Boston."

"Good, my name is Junior, I'm the boss boy here so you call me Master at all times, understand?"

Topha nodded.

"My cohorts are all trained warriors to protect wimps like you from the other lot, you call them Sir, understand?"

Topha was no wimp and was going to make that clear straightaway.

"I'm no wimp, they can kiss my ass before I call them Sir."

"Ok, no problem." Junior nodded.

Four boys were on Topha before he had time to react stripping him of his shorts. They pinned him face down and Junior nodded at the black warrior. He discarded his loincloth and fisted himself to an erection. Topha watched and then, as he moved round behind him he realized what was going to happen. He struggled like hell until someone grabbed his balls and squeezed hard. Result was compliance, but the scream as his anus was pierced by the black rod could be heard all over the island. He was fucked until the black stud orgasmed inside him, and then all of the warriors kissed an ass cheek before releasing him.

"They have all kissed your ass, now you call them Sir, but first, you thank Leo for putting you in your place, you'll be our fuck slut until we decide if you are worth something better."

Topha was almost traumatized by his ass fucking but did as he was told. He had never felt pain like he had just endured until his ass adapted to the invasion.

He eyed up Leo who looked older than the others.

"Yes Topha, take a good look. Leo is our champion, the oldest inhabitant of the island. He can fuck more ass in one session than anyone else, piss me off again and we will get him to try to beat his previous record, but just using you."

That was good enough for Topha. He was now determined to comply with any order whatever it was. He didn't want that black monster roaming around inside him again.

Leo was a typical black with short tight curly hair, some hair on his chest and legs and in the center a cock that had to be a good ten inches long, maybe more. He had a good body and looked to be about thirty, odd as this was supposed to be 'Boy Island'

Stood again he felt too much shame to look at any of the other warriors. He was marched back to the enclosure and saw what was going to be his home for the next two years. It looked like a mediaeval village in England. He remembered from his history books what they looked like. Shown to a hut, he was introduced to another naked boy.

"Damian, look after the new boy. Clean him up and have him at my hut in two hours' time."

Damian scanned Topha with his eyes before speaking.

"I'm Damian, I see you were the same as me, got stroppy with the Master. I suppose Leo fucked you."

Topha looked at this boy and decided he was going to like him.

"Hello, I'm Topha, and you're right. A painful introduction to my new life."

"Well, I've got two hours to try and help you not get any more punishment. Come on, let's get you showered. The two things we have plenty of here are water and soap."

Damian was eighteen, the same as Topha, mixed race, medium build with a very prominent penis. Below the waist he was quite hairy but there was little above. Topha noticed the cock because it had started to get hard.

"Sorry Topha, I love colored guys, and you are pretty special to look at."

"Are you queer then?"

"Huh, everyone is queer on this island, or they're celibate, and there aren't many of them. Who do you think we are going to have sex with?"

Topha blushed. This was not what he expected at all.

"After we shower I have to give you lessons in how to suck cock unless you are already good at it."

"No way Jose, I don't suck cock."

Damian looked at this boy and wondered if he would be given to the Premier Clan.

"The Master will have you strung up and whipped before he lets Leo loose on you again unless you do as he asks. He will want you to give him a blowjob when I take you to him. If you aren't very good you will know pain like you've never known before."

Less and less Topha liked this place. He wanted to rebel again in the shower when Damian started washing his ass, particularly down the crack.

"I have to do this in case the Master wants to fuck you as well."

"I'm going to survive here Damian so I guess I have to go along with whatever they want."

Damian patted Topha's cheek. "Good boy, the better you are, the more likely they are to be gentle with you, but be prepared for a load of humiliation to start with as well as some pretty rough sex, and pray for a new boy to come quickly so that he can take your place."

Topha gave him a quizzical look.

"When a new boy arrives the existing fuck slut moves up the pecking order. I expect warriors will still fuck you and get blowjobs, but not gang bangs like you will get to start with. If you really measure up you might be invited to be a warrior, but you would have to be really good at unarmed combat and using a knife or spear."

"Mmm, I'm not bad at unarmed combat, I did Karate for four years, but my main love was archery. I'm a dab hand with a bow and arrow."

Topha was laughing as he said that, but Damian was surprised.

"Jeez, if you let the Master know that you will probably be invited into the warriors almost straight away. Archers are the cream of our army."

Damian liked the sound of that.

The hut was decently furnished, which surprised Topha because they were so basic on the outside. Damian got comfortable and then told Topha to get down and start licking his cock. It progressed from licking to sucking, just the head to start with, then down the shaft and onto the balls. The instruction was comprehensive and Topha soon realized that it wasn't as bad as he expected. He knew what he liked so he was halfway there without any instruction. It was just a matter of getting over the embarrassment of having another man's cock in his mouth. The action got him a hard on as well as it was really quite erotic.

"Change places Topha, I like your cock, I'm going to reciprocate, only I'm going to bring you to orgasm and swallow your cum. You must do the same when you blow any of the warriors or they'll beat you. Don't spill any either or you get a beating as well. No matter what you are asked to do, do it, and be enthusiastic, better lots of sex than a bruised body. When they fuck you, use your gluts to massage their cocks. They all love that. I'll show you sometime because I'd like you to fuck me."

Topha was almost overloading, he had never fooled around with boys, he hadn't had a load of experience with girls either, but at least he wasn't a virgin.

By the time he had to go to the warrior hut Topha was a more than adequate cocksucker. He had swallowed one lot of Damian's sperm to see what it was like. Not bad he thought, a little salty but not unpleasant. He knew he would be alright on that score when the time came. He had also taken Damian's more than adequate cock in a quick fuck.

"I've lubricated you well Topha and stretched you and that should help. I would like to make love to you properly when you return."

Damian took him to the warriors hut and told him to stand at the entrance and request entry, giving his name first.

"Topha Lewis requests entry to the warrior hut."

"Enter," was said and he walked in. The hut was quite well furnished, almost luxurious. This all appeared to be an anomaly to Topha, the boys apparently lived in comfortable surroundings.

"Master, Damian told me I should tell you that I am a competent archer as well as a Karate exponent."

Junior was really pleased and told Topha so.

"You will show me later, and if you are good your life here will get much better. Now, stand in the middle of the floor and open your legs wide, put your hands behind your head."

Topha liked the sound of the first bit, but not the next bit. He felt acutely embarrassed stood on display with all the warriors milling round, and it got worse as they started playing with him and stroking him, passing ribald comments to each other. He blushed furiously but still got a good solid erection.

"Our slut boy will be able to fuck some good ass if he becomes a warrior. This piece of man meat is very presentable."

The boy that said that was stood in front of Topha and smiling, Topha smiled shyly back at him. He was gentle and his hands felt so good.

"Thank you Sir, I hope I can please you as well."

Topha had no idea why he said that, but there was some spark between this boy warrior and himself.

"Even without him performing for us Junior, I think I want this fuck slut to sleep with me tonight."

The master nodded his assent and Topha looked surprised.

"My name is Esteban, Damian will show you to my room after you have eaten tonight."

Topha smiled more broadly.

"Thank you Sir."

"If he is to be your slut for the night Esteban, perhaps he should practice his sucking skills first on you."

Esteban grinned and sat in a spacious armchair said to Topha, "Now, kneel between my legs and see how excited you can make me, and then make me cum, shall we say in ten minutes."

A clock was placed so that Topha could see it and everyone else gathered round, it was difficult though to concentrate on Esteban with all the attention his body was receiving. He could feel fingers worming away inside his anus, and other hands playing with his cock and balls, some quite gently and erotically, others a bit rough. Esteban was very sexy though, a Latino boy, and very handsome. Topha tried very hard to please this boy, there was something about him. Esteban felt the same, he realized that Topha was concentrating very hard to give him good head. He stroked Topha's hair and spoke quietly to him giving him pointers as to how he could make the blowjob better, and how to control when he came. The result was a terrific orgasm. Esteban was so pleased after Topha had finished that he lifted his face, bent forward and placed a long loving kiss on Topha's lips causing him to gasp and his eyes to water. He dropped his eyes so that Esteban couldn't see the tears.

"Thank you Sir, I hope that pleased you."

"Junior, this boy is terrific, please let me have him after tonight."

Junior laughed.

"Ah, our only romantic has found a new love. Alright boys, one hour to tear him a new anus and then Esteban can take him. Call Damian back, we will use him for the rest of our pleasure tonight."

No more was said on the subject, but Topha was reeling under the sexual attacks on him for the next hour. The first was to give Junior a blowjob for his assessment. Satisfactory, so the games began.

"On your back slut, open your legs wide, pull them back and wide Leo, I want to fist him."

Topha was appalled as he felt more and more fingers spreading his anus and watched in horror as all of the others started wanking over him.

"Open your mouth slut, our first load is for your stomach from the top end."

An occasional cock would be put in his mouth to suck for a little while as the others all jacked off over him. He felt the pain as Junior's fist went over his sphincter. He was panting trying to regain control of his senses. The pain gradually died down and it felt amazing making his cock get rigid again.

"You've worked your magic again Junior. His prostate looks pretty sensitive."

Esteban leant in then and sucked Topha until the first boy shot a load straight into Topha's mouth. Junior pulled out then and replaced his fist with a good thick hard cock. Damian entered and was watching this performance. The warriors were like animals around a hunting carcass for an hour. He found it difficult to believe an anus could stretch as wide as they stretched Topha, in between fucking him hard. Topha couldn't say anything because his mouth was filled with cock as well, all the time. The final few minutes were spent putting Topha into loads of different positions to fuck him for a few strokes and then the finale. They took him outside and all pissed on him. Mostly over his groin and face, making him keep his mouth open and swallow everything that went in.

"We are going to keep Damian for some more sex Esteban, you can take your little slut."

Esteban helped Topha to the showers where he washed him gently. He gave him copious quantities of water and a mouth wash, stroking him and calming him down all the time. He was surprised that although very upset, his boy appeared to be functioning.

"Now I am going to make love to you Topha. Just lay back and enjoy."

Esteban was so loving and gentle, plus he was so sexy to look at, he just swamped Topha's senses, making him want to cry with the pleasure he was receiving. He wanted to reciprocate but Esteban wouldn't let him. When the final act took place he entered Topha very gently and with loads of lubrication because he knew the boy would be sore, but he came quickly leaving both of them speechless for ages.

"That was wonderful Topha, you are going to live here with me, ok?"

Topha nodded and sighed with pleasure. Here he could be the boy he wanted to be, outside he would be the hard nut, to survive.

The next day he had to prove his archery ability. He was awful because there was no balance to the bow and the arrows because they were all different in thicknesses and therefore weight.

"Not very good Topha," came from a very unhappy Junior.

"No and my bet is that none of your archers are particularly accurate. Give me 24 hours Master to use of your facilities and I will show you consistent accuracy and greater range for your arrows."

Curiosity killed the cat, so Junior agreed.

"Esteban, you look after him."

With that the archery range was empty apart from the two.

"Show me where you keep the material for bows and arrows Sir, and the tools you use to make them."

"You don't have to call me Sir anymore Topha, come with me."

In a small shed Topha saw lengths of wood for the bows and arrows and sharp knives to shape them, material for stringing and for flights for the arrows. He checked the entire wood pile and selected one piece which he then set to work shaping. Esteban was fascinated as a bow took shape, a thick round grip, notched near the top for an arrow to rest in, flat and tapered for the length both sides and notched near the top to take the string. All of that took several hours and Topha showed Esteban how to select the material for the flights. Next came the arrows and once again Topha whittled away at them until he had several the same length and thickness.

"I need some soft metal to weight the arrows and balance the bow Esteban, where could I find it?"

Esteban thought about it and then ran off, to return a few minutes later with some empty tins and a set of metal cutters. Topha was delighted.

"Perfect," he cried out, "Now watch." Very quickly he had shaped arrow heads which he clamped to the arrows, fixed the flights and checked weight and balance. Then he cut strips to wind round the end of the bow, he needed weight there, again for balance. Finally came the gut to string the bow. This he measured carefully after checking the flexibility of the bow. One bow and half a dozen arrows completed and he went back out to the range to check the accuracy. After a dozen shots he moved the target further away and did the same again, but before he started the second lot Esteban told him.

"That won't work Topha, we can never get the arrows to fly that far for more than the first few."

Topha shot and with the first arrow hit the target, with the remainder he got more accurate.

"That is fantastic, how did you do that?"

"Weight, Esteban, and balance. The metal at the ends of the bow gives me balance and the weighted arrows allow them to travel further more accurately."

"Ok, but that won't last, the bows get weaker quickly."

"Show me where you keep them."

The moment he saw the storage he knew the problem.

"You leave the bows strung so they lose their flexibility, see," and with that he unstrung his own bow. "Now it will be fresh and strong next time I string it."

That was a long day and Esteban told Topha not to say anything to Junior until he saw the demonstration the next day.

With the added length of the flight and the accuracy Junior was delighted.

"We must make you a warrior straight away and you will be responsible for making our bows and arrows, and for training the archers."

Topha was delighted, no more nasty sex, just loving sex with Esteban, and he thought, maybe the odd romp with Damian.

It was great the next day to have a breechcloth to wear. There wasn't much of it but it covered all the private bits. He felt quite important taking all the archers and showing them what he wanted.

"The first thing you need is good bows. When you have shaped your new one, you will keep it with you so that no one else uses it. With practice you will learn how much weight to add to the ends to get the balance you want. I will ask Junior to give us a warrior escort and we will go out into the jungle to collect the material for the arrows. We will only gather wood that is the same uniform thickness. Each of you will carry one piece that I will give you so that you get it right. Arrows can then be communal weapons, taking what you need when the time comes to use them in anger."

The other boys were impressed with the way Topha took charge and by the end of his first week on the island Topha had a squad of archers who could all hit the targets on a regular basis. Junior was delighted and made Topha a lieutenant.

Esteban sat Topha down in their room one day to tell him about the Premier Clan.

"They are mostly very hard nuts, incarcerated for murder and the like. We are pussies in comparison, armed robbery, persistent small time criminals, so the others prey on us. Junior and Leo both overstayed their sentence to sort us out and teach us to protect ourselves. The authorities think that Leo is dead so he can stay forever. Junior smacked a guard at one of the changeovers and received an on the spot extension of one year. Now we have a small army that can defend themselves, but the others still try to capture some of us. Open attacks are rare, but we have to beat them off. With your archers we now have the chance to do it with no, or very few casualties. The authorities don't mind if we kill each other, as far as they are concerned we are beyond redemption anyway so we are doing society a favor. The worst thing that can happen to you is that you are captured. They would send you back to us, a bit at a time until we had all of you."

Topha didn't like the sound of that.

Chapter 2

The Premier Clan did decide to mount a raid sometime after Topha had finished training his archers and took Esteban as his second in command. The gang thought if they attacked from two sides they would have a better chance of penetrating the defenses of the enemy so when the alarm sounded Topha split his force. Because of the extra range of the archer's arrows they decimated the enemy before they were even within the old range that they were used to. When they kept coming on Topha's side he showed his archers how it was done. He was being fed arrows as fast as he could fire them and hit with everyone. The enemy retreated, taking with them the wounded from the first flight of arrows, but leaving the ones closest to the stockade. Topha insisted on taking a section of archers and a bunch of the non-warriors to bring in the wounded. Junior objected but Topha insisted they couldn't leave the boys out there to die. He eventually won and six badly wounded enemies were brought into the stockade under close guard.

"I don't care what you say Topha, they are to be secured and guarded, do what you like with them but I want them out of the stockade by nightfall."

Arrows were removed from bodies and the wounds dressed. Topha made sure they were all comfortable and guarded properly before going to Junior and making a suggestion.

"If I go to the enemy camp and tell them they can have their six wounded back, as soon as I appear in the clearing with them, will you put the wounded outside the gates and let them be recovered unmolested?"

Nobody wanted to see Topha do that, but he insisted. He wasn't particularly brave but he couldn't sit by and watch the enemy boys die.

He was shaking as he drew near the enemy camp and walked in unmolested until someone realized he was a stranger. They roughed him up a bit before he got to see their leader.

"I am called Topha, a lieutenant in Junior's army. We have six of your warriors in our compound. Their wounds have been dressed and they are accommodated on litters. If twelve of your men come with me we promise you safe passage and you can pick up your men from outside the stockade, unmolested and bring them back here."

The leader looked Topha up and down, indicated for his men to strip him.

"I think a better idea is for your men to bring them here, to help them make the decision we will start sending you back to them a piece at a time."

"That won't do you any good. I'm not important enough to sacrifice any of our men, and Junior made it clear I was on my own and if I didn't come back they would simply make a funeral pyre of your men just outside the stockade."

"So you are stupid then to come here."

Topha nodded. "Probably, but I couldn't stand by and see your men killed without trying to save them."

"Well stupid boy, we will have some fun with you before roasting you over an open fire."

Topha was strung up and several of the gang pleasured him, taking turns to fuck him. After a little while he received twenty strokes of a paddle that stung like hell and made him gasp.

Finally, they strung him between two poles and placed him on a rack over a fire pit. It was a charcoal pit and Topha realized he was actually going to be slow roasted. He realized the pain would be intense for ages before he was burnt unconscious. The tears were of self-pity. He had misjudged the enemy leader. He thought that getting six men back would be accepted. The heat had just started to be felt when a bucket of water was thrown over the charcoal and he nearly suffocated with the steam rising from the pit, and then a voice spoke.

"My brother is one of the wounded Dwayne, I would like him back. This little cocksucker isn't worth him, or the other five, let him go and I'll take eleven others to pick up the litters."

"You're very brave all of a sudden Jessie."

"No, I just think it's time that some humanity was brought into this camp and my brother is a good candidate to be the first to see it."

Dwayne could see he was likely to have a divisive fight on his hand if he forced the issue so he took a vote and was surprised that nearly everyone voted for the rescue. Jess took Topha for a bath and pampered him. The two boys realized that they liked each other.

"I'm Topha Lewis and I come from Boston. I have about eighteen months left to do."

"I'm Jess Conrad and I come from New York. I might be able to leave in two more years."

"When you get off the island, give me a call, my Dad is in the phone book, same initial as me."

"Are you a queer boy Topha?"

Topha grinned, "I thought we all were on this island."

"Well I am, always have been. I'd like to make love to you."

Topha was surprised but grinned. "I think I'd like that."

They talked animatedly as they walked back to the stockade. At the edge of the clearing Topha hailed the wall.

"We'll come in to collect the litters in two separate trips Junior so that half the bearers can cover the other half. Will you put the litters outside the wall?"

Jess noted how carefully the action was carried out. Archers manned the walls to guard the litter bearers who brought out the litters and put them down about twenty yards clear of the stockade.

"I'll walk in with your men Jess on each trip."

The action went like clockwork, Topha and Jess shaking hands and saying goodbye half way across the clearing before returning to their own side.

Junior wanted to hear all the details of the trip and Esteban wanted to know about Jess. He had noticed the warmth between the two boys.

"No stockade Junior and no guards, they must be supremely confident."

"So we could get in real close with archers and decimate their force before we were discovered and then just run like hell back here."

"Yeah, I guess we could, but I think you might find a different attitude now. Their leader is the hard ass, but there is a strong element for more humane thinking. My guess is that if we leave it they will come to us to normalize relations."

"Don't be daft Topha, they're animals, they won't change."

Topha shrugged, there was no point in arguing he could prove nothing. In his hut with Esteban afterwards he got the third degree.

"You had something going with the guy you came with from the Premier Clan didn't you?"

Topha laughed, "I could do I reckon, he's cute, and not an animal at all. His brother was one of the wounded, which was why he led the litter party. He had to stop the leader roasting me alive and then persuade eleven guys to come with him to carry their wounded back. The leader was going to leave them here to burn while they roasted me. The guy is gay and said he fancies me. There you are you have it all now, except the important bit. I love you Esteban, I think you are the best thing that's happened to me in a long time, but Jessie would be nice to have as a friend."

Esteban wasn't sure if Topha was telling the whole truth so continued.

"If this Jessie was here now, would you have sex with him?"

Topha thought about it and looked at the expression on Esteban's face as he replied.

"Mmm, if he was willing, but only if you were here as well. A threesome with him would be very exciting I think, particularly if we made love and didn't just have sex."

Esteban laughed then.

"Six months ago you had never indulged in boy/boy sex, now you are proposing an orgy."

Topha was giggling as he replied, "Yeah, but only a little orgy, maybe we could go for a big one when I have more experience."

Esteban couldn't win this so he did the only thing he knew to slow Topha down. He pounced on him and tumbled him onto their bed burying him in kisses and groping his groin. He was correct, Topha had become so enamored with boy sex he just melted as Esteban made exquisite sensual love to him.

"Oh, Lover, I think you have just taken me to Paradise. I love you Esteban, I hope we can make a life together after we get off the island."

Esteban was so pleased because he was feeling the same thing. He wanted to be with this friend and lover for a long time.

The warriors continued to train; particularly the archers, and Topha ran competitions to keep them enthusiastic. Several new boys arrived on the island and were used as prizes. Topha also ran Karate classes to help the boys become adequate at self-defense. At the end of his first year Topha watched several of the boys pack up to leave, Junior amongst them.

"Topha, you have proved yourself to be a brave and resourceful warrior. We must take a vote on my replacement as the overall leader and I am proposing you."

Only one other warrior was proposed and that was Esteban.

"I will vote for Esteban." Topha said.

"I will vote for Topha." Esteban said and they fell into each other's arms laughing.

The remainder of the warriors voted and Junior had to cast his vote to break the deadlock.

"Look after our family Topha."

Topha thanked Junior and turned to the remainder of the warriors.

"I take Esteban as my first lieutenant and make him commander of the archers. All other lieutenants please remain at your posts."

There were cheers all round and Topha detailed an escort of bowmen and lancers to escort the leaving boys to the landing beach, going with them. On the way back they ran into a crew from the Premier Clan doing the same thing. Under normal circumstances it would have meant a pitched battle, but Jessie was leading the other escort group. The two groups looked ready for confrontation when Topha realized the other leader was Jessie. They fell into each other's arms and hugged.

"I have thought of you often friend. We should have that meeting to make our lives together friendlier. We can do that now. Dwayne was killed in a stunt and our new leader is not so aggressive. If your leader feels the same we should progress that liaison."

Topha laughed. "I am the new leader and I would like that. Why don't you talk to your leader about it and come to the fort under a flag of truce which I promise to honor."

The parting was without any fighting and it was only a couple of days later that a small party appeared at the edge of the clearing under a flag of truce. Topha went to meet them with just four lancers as escort. Jessie was the leader of the party and embraced Topha warmly.

"My leader won't come to your fort so we need a neutral meeting place. I have suggested halfway across this clearing. It is the widest cleared space on the island and we can sit with a small negotiating party and our whole armies the same distance apart."

"I agree. We are closest so I will have table and chairs set up under an awning and we will supply food and drink for the meeting if it goes on for very long. And Jessie, I swear you needn't bring your whole army. We will honor the truce, even if it will be just you and your leader came."

"I will tell our leader. Let's plan for the leader and three lieutenants to be in the negotiating committee. The remainder of the escort will be up to the leader."

The two friends were so pleased that there was a good chance peace would reign on the island and that they would soon be able to socialize. Topha took Jessie aside to tell him about Esteban.

"I hope we can become good friends here, and when we leave the island, but I must tell you that I have a lover who I hope to live with when we leave here."

Jessie looked disappointed.

"I should have guessed. You are so good, and kind, it was only natural you would have a lover."

They parted, still friends and with a date three days ahead set for the meeting.

On the day Jessie emerged from the jungle alone and walked to the awning in the center of the clearing where he could see the table and chairs. Almost instantly, the gates of the fort opened and Topha walked out reaching the awning at the same time as Jessie. They embraced and kissed chastely showing friendship rather than love.

"It is so good to see you again Jessie. I hope you are not alone."

Jessie laughed. "No my friend, but my leader is not as trusting as me. He wanted me to see if it was good."

"It is Jessie. I will signal for my three lieutenants to join us and then walk back with you to bring your leader to the table."

Jessie looked surprised.

"We could capture you and take you back to our camp then with no problem."

"Yes, you could, particularly as I am unarmed."

Jessie shook his head wondering at his friend's foolhardiness.

They walked together to the edge of the clearing where another four of the Premier Clan waited. They were even more surprised than Jessie had been when he introduced them.

"Topha, this is our leader, Dominic."

They shook hands and then Jessie completed the introductions.

They started the walk back together, all unarmed, watching the equally unarmed lieutenants from the fort. Introduction completed and Topha noted the wary look exchanged by Esteban and Jessie.

"You two had better become friends or I am going to be very upset."

Topha was grinning as he said it and was followed by Jessie and Esteban who hugged each other.

"Well, our first lieutenants look set to be friends, Dominic, let's hope we can be as well."

Dominic was more reserved than Jessie so the atmosphere was a little strained to start with.

"What exactly do you expect from this meeting Topha?"

"Mostly, I expect a peace treaty. Whatever crimes we committed in our homeland doesn't need to be repeated here. I know you think we are pussies because our crimes were minor compared to most of yours, but we have proved a match for you in battle, and physically we are your equals. It makes no sense for us to continue our enmity on this island. Many of you are here for life, or until moved to adult facilities. You should be able to live in peace here as well."

"And what do we do to achieve that?"

Topha thought about this.

"How about a one month truce. During that time none of us leave our respective camps armed. That will allow us to roam and explore the island. There is no telling what pleasures we may find. If there are no major incidents in that time we reconvene here to hash out a permanent peace."

"What do you mean unarmed and major incidents?"

Topha laughed.

"Yeah, unarmed is a bit silly isn't it if there are wild animals on the island. Ok, armed for hunting but not for battlefield action. We have fights between ourselves sometimes, we don't all like each other and I expect that could happen if we interact with you. I wouldn't want this truce to end because one of you has a fight with one of us, as long as no weapons are used."

That appeared to satisfy all parties.

"I think it would be a good idea for Jessie and Esteban to set up a weekly meeting to hash out any minor problems that arise. They can sort out a mutual meeting place between themselves."

Jessie and Esteban nodded their agreement and the meeting broke up with Topha and Dominic shaking hands.

Walking back to the compound Esteban voiced what all the lieutenants were thinking. "I wonder if they will keep their word."

"I hope so," was Topha's quick reply, "We don't really want to spend our time on the island in a state of conflict do we?"

The weekly meetings between Esteban and Jesse worked well. Topha had predicted correctly that there would be minor scuffles between individuals, but nothing serious and at the end of the trial period a permanent peace treaty was signed quite formally by the two leaders and their lieutenants.

During the next few months, integration took on an even better state. Friendships became more serious and members of the Premier Clan took up almost permanent occupation in the fort, and vice versa as love blossomed.

The biggest change in circumstances occurred with Topha, Esteban and Jesse. The meetings of the two lieutenants had blossomed into a proper friendship and eventually a sexual liaison that pleased them both. Topha wanted a sexual relationship with Jesse but didn't want to lose Esteban. Esteban picked up on Topha's dilemma in conversation and talked it over with Jesse. The result was that Esteban and Jessie got Topha in the bedroom and made love to him together.

"Oh God, you two, what have you done to me?"

Topha had never orgasmed so intensely in his life, not just once, but in each of the other's rectums.

Esteban was grinning and Jesse answered.

"We've just shown you that we think a threesome can work without jealousy. I knew from the start that I was going to fall in love with you, Topha, and as Esteban and I met more often I realized I was falling for him as well. Esteban realized you felt the same about me so it just appeared logical to see if we could do this with joy and not jealousy. I think we can if you agree."

The threesome developed during the next few months with a load of threesomes, but remarkably many one on ones without jealousy rearing its ugly head. The three boys were open with one another making the liaisons easy.

Topha and Dominic set up a court system made up of one lieutenant from each side to pass judgment on disputes. They were few and far between, and punishments were made amusing for the benefit of both groups, usually carried out at a party in either camp.

Almost exactly one year from the first meeting of the two leaders a major event took place. A landing was made by troops who escorted a bevy of attorneys and three judges. The troop commander got hold of Topha and Dominic and the reason for the visit was explained.

"We have been following your activities on satellite link. This last year you have proved that you can integrate and be a cohesive social group. It has, therefore, been decided that each of you should be allowed to put a case before the judges to have your sentences commuted and be allowed to return to society. Those that don't make it this time will be given another chance in one year's time. To qualify for release you have to demonstrate that violence will now be eschewed in your lives."

The boys were all shocked at this possible reprieve and looked at Topha, Dominic, Esteban and Jesse who had been sensible enough to bring the two groups together.

Topha, Jesse and Esteban were the first three to be seen by the judges and were totally blown away when the decision on their cases were delivered together.

"You three demonstrated a maturity way beyond your years in bringing the feuding to an end. You have also demonstrated a love for each other that has allowed you to prosper in your relationship as a trio, most unusual. The decision of this court is that you are to be repatriated to a state that is gay friendly in its laws and you will be placed in college where your degree course will be paid for. Accommodation will be off campus so that you can continue to live together, much as you do now. Provided you work hard and obtain good degrees your parole period will end and you will be able to make your own decisions concerning your lives. This case is closed."

The boys were almost dumbstruck, but Topha managed to speak before they left.

"What about Dominic?"

The judge smiled at Topha.

"I think you three will need to do a lot of hugging when the decision on that young man is handed down."

All of the boys' records were with the visitors and the lawyers settled down individually with the boys to prepare a case for the judges. In some cases the meetings were short because the decision had often been made before the studies even started. Some boys were considered too new to the island for a decision to be made in their favor and they were informed that they would have to wait a year.

Dominic was one such individual. He was, of course, enormously disappointed but the three others hugged him and assured him they would be waiting for him when he was released next year.

The upside of that was that one of the original signatories to the peace would be on the island to see a new regime take over, hopefully peacefully.

Epilogue

The three boys did leave the island with many others and the visitors. They went home to see their parents and leave again almost immediately to take up their places at college. The love they had for each other continued to grow and always cognizant of the opportunity they had been handed, studied hard and loved just as hard.

One year later they were delighted to be joined by Dominic who had made the grade with flying colors, keeping the peace on the island and breaking in a new leader to keep the program on track.

They became an almost inseparable foursome, except when Dominic had a girlfriend. He had been the only 100% straight male they had come across on the island, never indulging in boy/boy sex.

Graduation four years later saw the boys taking places with social services to try to rehabilitate other young men before they went too far off the rails. Their own experiences being a major factor in the reason they were so good at their jobs.

Nothing changed very much for them as they got older. The only notable reminder of their island time was to attend Dominic's wedding the year after he graduated.

The End

Here is a sample from another story you may enjoy:

PACIFIC
Beach
HOT GAY EROTICA

Chris Johns

MAX hadn't noticed it before, but hanging from the beams that supported the roof were two ropes with loops on the end and a chain hoist in the center. His wrists were placed in the loops and the ropes pulled up. Because of their position on the beam the ropes spread Max's arms very wide, a spreader bar was used on his ankles so that he was now secured in a star position. He wasn't uncomfortable, but he felt embarrassed all over again as the four looked at him before setting about getting lunch. Kolby brought sandwiches to him and fed him.

He was talking to him softly and caressing his body, particularly his groin area. Max couldn't believe that this boy was being so gentle and caring.

When they we all fed and watered Kolby whispered to Max, "I won't be able to stop the guys all fucking you but I will try to stop them punishing you when the time comes for them to get rough."

Max didn't like the sound of that, just the five slaps had been very painful and he didn't want to think what ten with a cane would be like.

The boys released Max's wrists and laid him on the floor before hooking the spreader bar to the central chain and hauling it up so that his shoulders were still on the floor, but his anus was about twelve inches clear. Merrick and Zeke knelt either side of him and at a nod from Eddie, they pulled his cheeks apart as far as they could, opening up his anus for Eddie to poke around in it for a few minutes. He then took several of the large cushions off the furniture and put them under Max's lower back.

"Lower the bar Kolby until we can pull the slut a bit further forward forcing his knees down to his shoulders."

The others could see immediately what that achieved. It opened Max up even further.

"Kolby, you love this guy, take my place here and pleasure his anus and his cock and balls while I get some toys."

Kolby was torn, he wanted to play with Max because he thought he was so sexy, but he didn't want to embarrass him by doing it in front of the others. He knew he had no choice though and knelt at Max's ass and started to play. Despite the humiliation Max couldn't help but get an erection. Zeke and Merrick joined in then concentrating on Max's rectum, spreading it even wider and finger fucking him jointly. Eddie returned with a bag which he dropped by the side of Max, and he told Kolby to move. Taking his place Eddie opened the bag and pulled out a cock ring. He fastened it round Max making the comment that now he could stay hard all day. Next came a dildo that made everyone gasp. Kolby was almost crying as he begged Eddie not to use that on Max. Max looked in horror at the monster Eddie was waving about.

"I have been keeping this in reserve, hoping that one day we would find a slut to take it. It's nine inches round and fourteen inches long. From the tips of my fingers to just below my elbow is fourteen inches, but my forearm gets to ten and a half inches round. Game plan is that he takes both before we let him go."

Merrick was almost bouncing with glee looking at the monster and at Max's ass.

"I want to go first trying it," and Eddie laughed.

"Ok Merrick, you can go for the first six inches, open him up as much as you can first though."

Eddie and Zeke sat and watched as Merrick, using lots of lubricant opened Max up getting to the last knuckle on his hand before finger fucking him with all five digits, rotating them all the time. After ten minutes he tried opening the fingers out once they were inside Max. It looked amazing and Eddie disappeared again returning with a camcorder.

"Start again Merrick, with just one finger and increase to where you are now."

Kolby was crying and stroking Max's torso, whispering calming words to him, but Max was almost fixated on watching the action at his lower regions. When he saw Merrick reaching for the gel and the dildo he started to sweat and begged them not to fuck him with the dildo.

Eddie grinned at him, "Hey, you'll be in the Guinness book of records after today. We'll measure the dildo on camera and watch it penetrating you all the way, and then do the same thing with my arm before I go in as well."

When Merrick was ready, he placed the head of the dildo at Max's anus and told him to relax. Max did the opposite and used his muscles to tighten up his anus. That didn't work because Merrick and Zeke plastered his butt with ten very hard slaps before Merrick pushed hard and got the glans over Max's sphincter. The pain made his eyes water, but Merrick had done such a good job of opening him up that it was tolerable. Everyone watched as Merrick saw Max's reaction and proceeded to bury the first six inches in Max's ass…

If you enjoyed this sample then look for **Pacific Beach.**

Also by this Author:

Brotherly Love

Underworld

Revenge of the Jocks

Indian Abduction

Pleasurable Abduction

Lost

A Grip in Deep

Bullet Holes

Gay Porn Star

Delightfully Yours

Embracing the Greener Side

Promotional Desire

Aviator's Hidden Turbulence

Almost Paradise

The Hardcore Remedy

Relish Pretender

Doctor Boner

Captivated Attractions

Academically Horny

Flight of the Hornies

From the Author

If you want any more info about me, please feel free to ask! I'm a very open person so you won't offend me if you want to get more personal.

If you'd like to give me comments or suggestions to any of my books, feel free to shoot me an email at chris_johns@awesomeauthors.org.

Check my page on Amazon and my blog for Updates and interesting info.

Author Central – http://amzn.to/185Sar5
Author Blog - http://chris-johns.awesomeauthors.org/

If you enjoyed any of my books then please share the love and click like on my books in Amazon.

If you write me a review and send me an email I will send you a free book, or many.
(Just know that these emails are filtered by my publisher.)

Good news is always welcome.

One Last Thing, For Kindle Readers...

When you turn the page, Kindle will give you the opportunity to rate this book and share your thoughts on Facebook and Twitter. If you enjoyed my writings, would you please take a few seconds to let your friends know about it? Because... when they enjoy they will be grateful to you and so will I.

Thank You!

Chris Johns
chris_johns@awesomeauthors.org

About the Author

The author has drawn from his lifetime experiences as a Marine Engineer and Helicopter Pilot to take his readers round the world with his erotic stories.

Born in a small town in middle England he joined the Royal Navy straight from school and spent four years at engineering college before going to sea. After promotion to first engineer he took a career turn and trained as a helicopter pilot. The move afforded him huge opportunity to travel both as a Naval Pilot and later as a Commercial Helicopter Pilot. His Bio Pic was taken when he was relaxing in his company's social club, serving his fellow pilots and engineers with some excellent English Ale.

Retired now in the Caribbean he took up writing to compliment his other great love, sailing.

www.ingramcontent.com/pod-product-compliance
Lightning Source LLC
Chambersburg PA
CBHW071352130626
46556CB00005B/2155